# AVALANCHE!

# AVALANCHE!
## by Ron Roy

*illustrated by Robert MacLean*

A Unicorn Book
E. P. Dutton   New York

*for Emilie McLeod, a very special person*
*R. R.*

Text copyright © 1981 by Ron Roy
Illustrations copyright © 1981 by Robert MacLean

*Library of Congress Cataloging in Publication Data*

Roy, Ron, date    Avalanche!
(A Unicorn book)

Summary: Upset over his parents' impending divorce,
fourteen-year-old Scott goes to visit his older brother
in Colorado where they are both buried by an avalanche.
[1. Avalanches—Fiction.  2. Divorce—Fiction.
3. Colorado—Fiction]
I. MacLean, Robert, date   II. Title.
PZ7.R8139Av  1981  [Fic]  81-2224
ISBN 0-525-26060-9         AACR2

Published in the United States by Elsevier-Dutton
Publishing Co., Inc., 2 Park Avenue, New York, N.Y. 10016

Editor: Emilie McLeod    Designer: Janice Ferro

Printed in the U.S.A.   First Edition
10 9 8 7 6 5 4 3

# Contents

# 1

## White Night

Scott Turner stared out the round window of the small plane. He saw only white. It was snowing, his pilot said, "like the inside of a down pillow." Scott didn't know how they'd ever land, but that wasn't *his* problem. He had enough of his own.

Like what do you say to a brother you're about to see for the first time in years? Tony had left home six years ago when Scott was eight. He just drove out of town one day with some clothes and two hundred dollars.

Scott's parents had surprised him with a week's vacation in Aspen, Colorado, to visit Tony. Then they hit him with surprise number two: they were getting a divorce. End of family. Nice knowing you. They'd spend a few days in St. Thomas, working out the details, then fly back to the States for the divorce.

And good old Scott would have a wonderful time in colorful Colorado while they decided where he'd live when he came back.

It had gotten dark. The snow swirled around the plane like the thoughts in Scott's head. The pilot's voice shattered the silence: "Seat belts, please; we'll be landing in Aspen, Colorado, in seven minutes."

Scott cinched his belt and sat back. He was scared. He closed his eyes, dug his nails into the foam arms of his seat. The wheels hit the ground before he realized they were landing. Sweat ran in cold streams down his sides. He'd made it.

Snow pelted Scott as he jumped from the open hatch of the small plane. His legs felt weak and his whole body was stiff from the cramped seat. Shielding his face with one hand, he peered into the darkness around him. The snow made seeing beyond ten feet impossible.

Suddenly someone appeared in front of him, like a genie out of a bottle. Broad shoulders, ski hat yanked over his ears, full beard. All covered with snow. A walking snowman built like a bear. Tony? No, not unless he'd put on a lot of weight.

"Welcome to sunny Florida." The bear laughed, hoisting himself in through the hatch. In a minute Scott's pack, skis and boots were shoved out. "These yours? Anything else?"

"No, that's all," Scott said. He took his gear from the outstretched hands and set it in the snow.

"Can't leave it there, kid," the voice said from inside. "Got a ton of other stuff to unload." Then as if reading Scott's mind, he added, "You being picked up? Waiting room's straight ahead."

Again Scott tried to see through the blinding snow. This time he made out a glow in the darkness. Throwing

2

his skis and boots over one shoulder, he trudged toward the light, dragging his pack in the snow.

The outlines of a low building emerged from the murk. Beyond that Scott saw only night and snow. He might have been in Siberia. He remembered the massive airport in Denver. Had he landed there only a few hours ago?

The door to the waiting room was stuck and wouldn't open. Great, thought Scott. I'll freeze to death right here. They'll fly me home in a cake of ice. He laughed to himself. There wasn't anyone there to pay the mailman.

He applied his shoulder to the door, and he was suddenly inside, pack, skis, snow and all. It was a square place built of cinder blocks, with plastic chairs, an office, a phone booth and two machines that took money and gave back food. That was it. No people. No Tony.

Scott crossed the room and tapped lightly on the office door. Nothing. He tapped again, harder. A crash made him jump back, away from the door. The noise came from behind him. Whirling, he saw the friendly snow bear and the pilot dragging big cartons into the room. Snowflakes the size of quarters flew into the room around them.

"Looking for me?" the bearded man asked, showing a lot of teeth through his jungle of hair. The pilot stamped snow from his boots and disappeared through a door Scott hadn't noticed.

"My brother was supposed to meet me," Scott said. "He lives in Aspen and he . . ."

Scott never finished. The door crashed open again and

3

he recognized his brother. Even through the padded jacket, ski cap and faded jeans, it couldn't have been anyone else. Six years hadn't erased the proud stance, the eyes that tried to take in everything at once. And the restlessness. Like he wanted to get this reunion stuff over with and get on with his life.

"Howdy, little brother."

"Hi, Tony." Scott didn't know what he expected to happen next. On the plane, he'd barely been able to picture his brother. He certainly hadn't planned what he was going to say to him. Two identical pairs of blue eyes checked out the owner of the opposite pair.

"Motor's running," Tony said finally. "This your gear?" he asked, indicating with his toe the pack at his feet.

"Those skis, too, against the wall. And the boots."

"You a skier, little brother?" Tony's voice betrayed a little more interest.

"Not really; Dad bought them for me. He thought I . . ."

"Turn you into a downhiller in no time," Tony interrupted, laughing too loudly. "Let's get going before we have to sleep here."

Then Scott was in the night again, squinting to keep the snow out of his eyes. "Throw the skis in the back," Tony yelled over the hood of the pickup. "We'll squeeze your pack up front."

Scott couldn't believe his eyes. It was the same old Ford Tony had driven back home. Seeing it made Scott feel a little better, not such a foreigner in this land of hairy giants and never ending snow.

"How far is Aspen?" Scott asked, shivering.

"About three miles straight ahead. Be there in three minutes."

Shocked, Scott turned to look at Tony. How could he drive sixty miles an hour in this stuff?

Tony burst out laughing. "On a dry day, I mean. Relax, Scottie, relax."

Scottie. That was the first time Tony had called him by his name. It sounded good. Scott smiled in the darkness of the truck cab and closed his eyes. And dozed.

# 2

## *Blue Morning*

Scott opened his eyes, then closed them again fast. Tiny pinpricks of sunlight warmed his eyelids. In his dream he had been in a blizzard, floundering waist deep in quicksandlike snow. Was the light part of the dream?

He tried opening his eyes again, this time peeking through slits. The light was still there. And something blue, fresh as a bluebird's wing. He opened his eyes a little more. It was morning; sun and sky were welded together outside a window. What window? He sat up, rubbed his eyes, looked around him.

Tony's apartment. He was in Colorado, in bed. He snuggled back into the covers and checked out the apartment he'd slept in.

This was the living room, and he was on the sofa. There was a big, stuffed chair opposite him. A stereo setup with speakers as big as coffins took up a whole corner of the room. Tony and music were never far

7

apart. Tapes, hundreds of them, were stacked everywhere. Most of the wall space was covered with posters: ski shots of guys hotdogging over cliffs; hot-air balloons hovering near mountainsides; canoes shooting impossible rapids.

A counter separated the living room from a kitchen that looked almost big enough to turn around in. To the right, a half-opened door revealed a fur-covered toilet seat. Scott chuckled. Another opened door showed that Tony was no longer in his bed.

It wasn't much, but Tony never had cared where he dropped his boots. This place had all he needed. It was home for Tony.

Home. Scott's own home back in Connecticut was falling apart. Would he ever have a real home again? Or would he have to run away, as Tony had, to find it?

Where is Tony? Scott wondered. They'd come in last night, dumped Scott's gear and gone right out again for hamburgers. They had gone to the Chart House, where Tony worked, and made their own. No McDonald's for Tony Turner.

They'd had fun. The waiters and cooks had teased Tony about being too cheap to take his brother out and pay for his meal. But they all liked Tony and called him T, for his first and last initial. And they'd been waited on, even in the kitchen. Half-inch slices of cheese for their hamburgers; extra tomatoes for the salads. And pieces of cheesecake that took courage to finish.

Tony's job was headwaiter. That was like being manager without a manager's pay, Tony had explained. But it allowed him to wait on tables where the real money was. Scott had stared as a few of the waiters counted their tips in front of him. "Forty," he heard one mutter. "Oh, well, it's only Tuesday." Forty dollars in tips!

Tony must have seen Scott's eyes bulging, because he laughed out loud, splattering part of his sandwich. "These clowns take in over a hundred on Saturday nights, little brother."

Some quick multiplication told Scott that a waiter could earn two or three hundred dollars a week! He thought about the bills in his own pocket: spending money from his father. He had twenty-five dollars. Oh well, it was only Tuesday.

It was still snowing when they trudged home later. Tony told Scott the town of Aspen was shaped like a bowl stuck in the middle of the Rocky Mountains. It had been settled in the 1800s as a mining town for silver.

Back in the apartment, Tony had tossed Scott sheets and a blanket. They'd made up the sofa together, and that was all Scott could remember.

At least he had gotten undressed, Scott discovered now as he climbed out from under the blanket. He stood in his underwear and the socks he'd worn from home. He found a note on top of his jeans:

> Howdy!
> Eggs and stuff in the fridge. I'm working today at C. House; stop in for lunch.
> Make yourself at home and enjoy.
>                                          Tony

Scott felt strange in this apartment. He hardly even knew Tony. Would they ever be brothers again?

Scott crumpled the paper into a ball and tried for two points in the sink. He missed. Laughing, he headed for the bathroom.

# 3

## *Tony's Promise*

By the time Scott had eaten and cleaned up the kitchen, it was ten thirty. He'd stashed his clothes in a drawer in Tony's room. He discovered that his brother wasn't a neat housekeeper. The unmade bed was a dumping ground for clothing not being worn at the moment.

The apartment was one of four in a small, dark brown building: two up and two down. Scott walked out onto the narrow balcony and stood in the sun. Tony was right; the town was shaped like a bowl. And all around it, crowding the sky, were the most beautiful mountains in the world. Covered with snow, they surrounded Aspen like guards.

The town itself was small, and Tony's apartment was on the eastern edge. Most of the buildings that Scott could see seemed in perfect condition, though most of them were over a hundred years old. The sidewalks, where cleared of snow, were brick. Vintage streetlamps and signs gave the town an old-West look.

Hundreds of people milled around with skis on their shoulders. Some wore hats and jackets, but most were in jeans and flannel shirts. It was actually hot out, like a September day in Connecticut. Scott peeled off his sweater and gloves. He kept his hat on, pulled the door shut, and walked down the stairs.

He found himself in an alley. Tony's truck was parked where they'd left it, and Scott realized he'd walked to work. The alley led into town, and Scott walked in and out of the shops with no destination. The people were friendly. They seemed ready to drop what they were doing to gossip and joke with each other. Skis stuck out of snowbanks like multicolored trees. Scott was enjoying himself. He almost forgot why he was in Aspen, and the fear that his parents didn't want him.

By the time his stomach told him to look at his watch, it was noon and a lot warmer. No one wore a hat, and Scott saw guys in tee shirts. He could feel his face growing tight in the sun, and loved it. A tan in March!

He found the Chart House easily, but would not have recognized it as a restaurant. It looked like someone's home. When he went in, a girl asked if he wanted lunch.

"I'm looking for my brother, Tony Turner," Scott said.

The girl smiled. "Oh, you're Scott. I heard you were coming. How do you like Aspen?"

"I haven't seen too much of it, but it's a pretty town," Scott said. "And the weather is great."

"I guess you're not a skier," the girl said.

"How did you know?"

"The skiers are mad because the ski patrol is shutting down most of the trails."

"Why?"

"Avalanches. It happens every year if we get heavy snow in November and December, especially if it turns warm, like now."

"I saw a lot of people walking around with skis this morning," Scott said. "Where were they all going?"

"Most of them didn't know the runs would be closed. A few will ski anyway, and take their chances."

"Leave it to my little brother to find the prettiest lady in Colorado on his first day here." Tony had come out of the kitchen in his waiter's uniform: Hawaiian shirt, blue corduroy pants, tennis sneakers. He slid an arm around the girl and nuzzled her neck. "So you've met my brother, Candy."

"He's real nice," Candy said, giving Scott a smile. "And much more polite than you." She dug her elbow into Tony's ribs.

Scott blushed. "She was telling me about the ski patrol shutting all the trails down. What will the skiers do?"

"Sit in the pubs and drink and gripe." Tony looked at Candy. "Did you tell Scott I'm taking the two of you skiing tomorrow on my secret trail?"

"Not me, T. I have to work. Besides, I heard they start dynamiting tomorrow. The patrol won't let anyone up there."

"They don't blast Smuggler," Tony said. "And who says you have to work? You can switch with Lois or Brownie."

"No thanks, Tony. I need the money." She looked at Scott, and she wasn't smiling anymore. "Are you guys really going skiing tomorrow?"

"We'll talk about it at lunch," Tony said. "If the hostess will find us a table."

Candy took them to a corner table, left menus and went back to her post.

"She's nice," Scott said, watching her walk away.

"Don't go getting any ideas," Tony said, pretending jealousy. "It took a year to get her to go out with me. No Easterner is cutting in."

Scott played the game. "But she flipped over me. I can't help it."

Tony roared and banged the table with his fist, grabbing the attention of the other diners. "What do you want to eat? It's on me," he said calmly.

"I've got money," Scott said. He looked down at the table.

"Hang on to it; you'll need it." Tony stared at Scott. "Something wrong?" he asked.

Scott blushed. "Tony, I don't really ski very well," he said, pretending to study the menu. "And if it's dangerous, maybe we . . ."

Tony cut in. "Don't worry, little brother. I promise everything'll be fine. Trust me. Okay?"

Scott felt uncomfortable. Anger crept up the back of his neck. "Okay," he muttered. "I won't worry."

Should he trust Tony? Scott remembered how Tony had disappeared that morning six years ago with no warning. He could feel Tony's eyes on him when the waiter asked for their order.

16

# 4

## *Skater's Warning*

It was a perfect day. From his sofa bed, Scott stared out the window at a cloudless, robin's-egg-blue sky. At eight o'clock, sunlight poured into the room. The peace was disturbed only by Tony's voice from the shower, booming: "My granny was a lady, though a little bit shady. . . ."

Scott smiled. Ten minutes ago he'd been awakened by a naked wild man, throwing pillows and shouting, "Out of bed, you lazy teenager! Where do you think you are, boarding school? UP! UP!" Before Scott could capture the pillows to heave them back, Tony was safe in the bathroom.

They were going skiing. Tony had compromised and borrowed two pairs of cross-country skis. "Just till you get your snow legs," he'd told Scott. "Then we'll chew up the trails!"

Scott wasn't sure about that, but he was glad he wouldn't have to downhill today. Cross-country skiing

17

was something he knew about. A bunch of the guys at school had cross-country skis and used them a lot. His roommate used them to get to some of his classes.

"Your turn." Tony was out of the bathroom, leaving wet footprints on his way to get dressed. "Hurry up. We're going to the Village Pantry for waffles. Let's get there before all the tourists wake up."

And they did. There were only two couples sipping coffee. They were locals, and Tony knew them. Everyone wore jeans. No one was in a hurry. Scott felt like he belonged.

A waiter sauntered over, yawning. "Didn't mean to wake you," Tony teased. "Meet my kid brother from Connecticut: Scott Turner, Dave Higgins. Affectionately known as Skater."

"Why Skater?" Scott asked.

Tony explained, grinning. "It's the weird way he skis. He puts one ski in front of the other and pushes himself along, like he's ice-skating. Any normal person would break a leg."

Dave laughed. "Your brother didn't get out of bed at this hour to listen to your lies, T. What're you guys having to eat?"

"Waffles for both of us, piles of them," Tony said, without checking with Scott.

"I'll have fried eggs," Scott said. "Do they come with toast?"

"You bet," Dave said. "We bake about ten different kinds of bread right here."

"I'll eat whatever kind you put on my plate," Scott said. "And orange juice, please."

"Coffee for me, Skater," Tony put in. Then he looked at Scott as if he were seeing him for the first time. "You don't like waffles?" he asked.

Scott felt hot under his jacket. He hadn't meant to contradict Tony, but he hadn't been able to stop himself. "I like waffles fine, Tony, but I like to choose my own food." There, he'd said it. He half expected Tony to blow up. Instead, Tony smiled.

"I'm sorry, kid, I just assumed. Forgive me?"

Scott smiled back. "Sure. But Tony? How about calling me Scott instead of kid?"

Tony's face hardened for an instant, then relaxed. "Check." There was a pause. "Now that you've put me in my place, tell me about this divorce."

Scott told him as much as he knew. And he was thinking: I want him to like me; he may be all I have.

Scott's eggs were done the way he liked them: flowing sunshine in the middle and crispy around the edges. Scott was mopping up with his toast as Dave came in from the kitchen.

"What gets you out of bed so early, T?" he asked.

"I'm taking Scott up to Smuggler. He's going to give me a lesson on touring skis in the meadow. Right, Scottie?"

Scott had a mouthful and couldn't answer.

"You've got to be kidding," Dave said. He looked from brother to brother. "They've closed the mountain."

Tony chuckled. "They've been closing all the mountains in March every year I've been here," he said. "They dynamite all the usual avalanche chutes, and the

tourists applaud like crazy when they hear the big *boom-booms*. But they don't blast Smuggler because most people ski Ajax; it's closer."

"Where's Smuggler?" Scott asked.

Tony pointed out the window over their heads. "Smuggler is on the other side of town, opposite Ajax. Plenty of places to use cross-country skis."

"If you get caught, you lose your free lift tickets," Dave said, starting to clear the table.

Tony clapped a hand on Dave's shoulder. "I'm not going to get caught, and I'm not going to get myself and my brother here dynamited off the planet, either," he said. "What I am going to do is buy us all a frosty beer at Little Annie's tonight. What time do you get off?"

"Five thirty."

"We'll be there," Tony said. "That is, if we ever get out of this tourist trap you call a restaurant."

Tony had his way and paid the bill. He seemed annoyed at Dave as they got into the truck. He skidded as he left the main drag.

"Can this old thing get up a mountain?" Scott asked. He hoped he could tease Tony out of his bad mood.

"I dropped the body onto a jeep chassis a few years ago. Your big brother now owns the only four-wheel-drive Ford in Colorado." He smiled. "There isn't a mountain in the Rockies that can stop us."

21

# 5

## *Avalanche!*

The old truck bucked and jerked noisily. Scott's teeth rattled. They'd been climbing over boulders and tree stumps for twenty minutes, but it seemed like a year. What was left of his rear end would be sore forever. No wonder Tony has a fur-lined toilet seat, Scott thought, sneaking a look at his brother.

Tony seemed to love it. He drove in a crouch with his bottom six inches off the seat. His feet and flexed knees absorbed the jolts before they got to his teeth, which was why he was able to chat all the way up the mountain and not risk biting his tongue off.

"Thousands of Chinese workers cut this pass about a hundred years ago. . . . Lot of silver came out of this mountain. . . . Look, a hawk, see him? . . . This is great, look at that sky!"

Scott saw no sky. His eyes were shut in order to avoid seeing the five-hundred-foot drop out his window.

Eight inches to the right was sure death. The truck would free-fall, then hit and burst into flames. Scott's father would save a fortune in tuition.

Tony turned, saw Scott and erupted in laughter. "Stand up, grab the dash, like this!" He demonstrated.

Scott tried it. It worked. He was able to stand in place, bent so that his head grazed the cab ceiling. He grinned, giving Tony a thumbs-up sign. "Thanks," he yelled over the engine.

Scott looked through the windshield. Sixty feet ahead of them the road seemed to end. On their left, a cliff climbing into space; on the right, a drop into eternity. And straight ahead, blue sky. Scott felt his breakfast eggs beginning an uphill climb toward his throat.

"HANG ON! SHARP CORNER!" Tony took his foot off the gas, whipped the wheel around, tapped the brake, then clutched and accelerated, all in one motion. There was road ahead of them again. They were saved. Scott stood frozen to the dash, a one-hundred-and-fourteen-year-old boy, white and shaking. He hardly knew when Tony swerved and stopped. "You okay?"

Scott lowered himself into his seat. He waited till his breakfast went back to where it belonged. "Piece of cake."

"You looked scared there for a minute."

"All your imagination."

"Good, because there's no way to turn around up here. We go down backwards."

Scott almost fell for it. He remembered how Tony had fooled him about driving sixty in a snowstorm at the airport. So he didn't turn on his brother, mouth agape, like a foolish kid. Instead, he flashed a smile and said, "Great! How about letting me drive?"

This time it was Tony whose mouth fell open. And Scott who burst into laughter. Then they were both howling, pounding knees and rocking the pickup.

"Got me, kid," Tony said finally.

"What?"

"Sorry, I mean Scott. It just slips out. When I left, you were a little kid, and all of a sudden you're grown up."

Scott blushed, felt himself growing taller right in the truck. Soon he'd burst his clothes, like The Incredible Hulk. "Where do we ski?" he asked, changing the subject.

"There's a meadow. I'll show you after I turn this rig around. If we get snowed on, I want to be headed in the right direction." He did a miraculous U-turn, parked, and stuck the keys over the visor.

Scott stepped out of the cab into a postcard of mountains and sky. The blue went forever, interrupted by snowcaps that looked close enough to touch. Scott tried, but was unable to keep himself from gaping. The air was cool and the sun was hot. And everything was so clear he could almost taste the view.

"I don't believe it," he whispered. "I just don't believe this really exists."

"This is what keeps me here, pal," Tony said. Then he thumped Scott on the back, breaking the spell. "Let's do some skiing."

25

They skied across a meadow of ice cream under a sky of velvet. Above them, upper Smuggler stood green, white, and majestic. The sweat ran down their backs beneath their clothing. They removed their jackets, tied them around their waists and continued in shirt sleeves.

They were in a magic land of snow, surrounded by millions of pine trees. They skied under a peak almost a half-mile high, but the top wasn't visible from where Tony and Scott stood.

Crags, like giant knuckles, interrupted the smooth, steep expanse on the side of the peak. And every inch was covered with snow.

"This is one of the most beautiful meadows in Aspen," Tony said, releasing a binding. "In the spring people come to camp and hike here from all over the country."

Scott understood why. He'd never seen anything like these mountains. They made him want to stand all day, just looking.

"How about some munchies?" Tony unzipped his pack and began removing tinfoil-wrapped hunks of bread and cheese. He'd also brought two apples and a thermos of orange juice. They sat on their jackets and ate in silence. Each was within his own daydream when they heard the first *boom*.

"What was that?" asked Scott.

"Dynamiters," Tony answered, chomping on an apple. "Over on Ajax. They're bringing down some of the snow while the people are off the slopes."

Scott looked around nervously.

"Don't worry, there's never been an avalanche here that I know of. See those trees going all the way up? If there'd been avalanches, there'd be a wide chute with not a tree standing. Relax."

After their snack they played baseball with the tinfoil and one of Scott's skis. They fell and tripped each other like children. They ate snow and stuffed it in each other's shirts. They flopped on their backs, making snow angels. Finally, exhausted, they lay still, faces turned upward, glowing. There had been other *boom*s, but they went unnoticed by Scott, ignored by Tony.

Scott was in heaven. It was as though he'd never lost Tony. He'd found him again, and his parents could do whatever they wished. He was where he wanted to be.

They dozed in the sun like worn-out puppies. Later, drunk from thin air and exercise, they slipped into their skis and started back. Then it happened. Scott's heaven was turned upside down and he found himself in hell.

There was no *boom*, no warning. Just particles of snow jumping in the air. A sudden breeze from nowhere. And then the rumbling. They were standing in the shadow of the mountain peak. Scott looked up first, then Tony.

What they saw above them was no longer a mountainside but a wave: a white wave, tumbling and plunging; a wave so huge that it seemed the whole mountainside had peeled off and was falling on their heads.

"AVALANCHE! RUN!" Tony was ten feet away, shouting. Scott couldn't move. He was made of ice. Tony reached him, shoved him forward and yelled

senseless words. Then Scott was skiing, falling, rising, skiing again. The snow was sucking at his legs. . . . It was his dream turned real. No matter how he tried, he could move only in slow motion. Fear rose in his throat, sour.

And then the avalanche hit him. It lifted him up gently, then flung him down fiercely; his feet flew from under him; the sky spun and was gone. Everything was gone except white turned red in the thundering fury of the wave that bore him on and on.

He was a swimmer, struggling to keep near the surface, but the tide was too strong. It threw him head over heels, flinging his arms and legs about as if he were a rag doll. He seemed to be spinning through space; suddenly he was yanked out of space by a gigantic hand that was crushing the life out of him.

Then nothing.

# 6

## *Buried*

Scott opened his eyes, and his lashes brushed against snow. It was very dark. He blinked, trying to see. He saw blackness. Fear gripped him. He didn't know where he was. He didn't know why he couldn't see. Was he blind? Or dreaming?

Then he felt the coldness, the silence. And he slowly remembered. Snow. He had been skiing, and tons of snow had plunged down the mountainside toward him and Tony. TONY! He tried to .yell. He was paralyzed with fear and could not utter a sound.

He understood the blackness and coldness. He was buried beneath the snow. And so, probably, was his brother. He began clawing at the snow. A mistake. The small pocket of air formed by one arm bent over his face disappeared. He was choking on snow. He stopped struggling. Slowly, with great care, he carved another space around his nose and mouth.

His heart pounded but his chest didn't move. The weight of the snow made taking breaths difficult. He was going to suffocate. He felt his stomach churn and send food rushing toward his throat. It took every bit of strength he had to swallow, getting rid of the bitter taste.

He had to think. If he tried to dig out, he might sink deeper. How long could he stay where he was? How long had he been there? He thought he could hear his watch. His arm was over his head, but he decided not to risk moving it to look. He didn't think he was hurt. What about Tony? Was he hurt . . . or dead?

Scott knew he had to try to get out, to take the risk. Tony was somewhere, and he had to get to him. He tried to think of everything he'd ever heard about avalanches, but drew a blank. He hadn't heard anything.

He was buried. This knowledge pounded at him, made him dizzy. Terror overcame him and he was insane. He screamed, kicked, clawed at the ice and snow. He felt his nails rip, but he was beyond pain. The snow shifted, and Scott screamed in panic. ''I DON'T WANT TO DIE! PLEASE, GOD, NO. PLEASE!'' He was crying, and his throat ached from the sobbing. Slowly his panic was cried away, and he was still.

He tasted snow and grit. His madness had gotten him nowhere. He made another breathing space, forced his body to relax. Panic can kill you. He knew that from lifesaving in school. He assessed. Where were his skis? Poles? Did he have anything in his pockets?

He had to know if his skis were still clamped to his

shoes. If they were, he'd have to release the bindings or he'd never be able to dig out.

He took a breath, held it, started moving his arms. An inch at a time, he pushed snow away from his body. Something creaked, and he felt new pressure on one hip. He froze. Please, not another avalanche. It was okay; he continued.

It took almost five minutes for Scott to discover that one ski was gone. The other binding had held, but the ski had snapped just above his shoe. He had half a ski, no poles, no gloves. And the blackness. If only he could see!

He was exhausted. Air was running out. He couldn't stay under too much longer. He'd fall asleep, freeze to death. It could happen; he'd read it in books. First you close your eyes, then you start to feel warm, drowsy. . . . "NO!" He began wiggling his fingers, blinking his eyes, anything.

That was when he felt the movement. He stopped, afraid of shifting snow. No, it wasn't like snow. Something touched his hand. Something warm.

Tony! Scott's heart thudded. Had some miracle tossed them together? Scott uncurled his cold fingers and gently reached out. He felt a twinge of pain in his chest. Was he hurt after all? Had he broken his ribs? He reached again, touched the thing. It wasn't Tony. Something small and soft was embedded in the snow near Scott's hand.

He felt, using his fingers for eyes. Cupping his hand, he forced it around the thing and pulled. When he had it near his chest, he examined it with both hands. It was an animal! A tiny, living, breathing animal.

It was small, like a mouse or chipmunk. He felt for a tail, found barely a stub. The ears, too, were tiny. The feet were miniature hands. The beating of the tiny heart against his thumb was the only movement Scott could feel. Whatever the creature was, it had been torn from its hibernating place by the avalanche. Now, like Scott, it was trapped under the snow. To freeze to death.

Not if Scott could help it. Groping with one hand, he found the zipper to his jacket and pulled. The buttons on his shirt were more difficult, because his fingers were numb. Finally one came free of its buttonhole, and he slid the animal inside. Its belly was against Scott's. He yanked the zipper up and moved his hand toward the broken ski.

He was not going to freeze to death. He was going to get himself out from under the snow and find Tony. Or die trying. The ski was as long as Scott's arm, jagged at the broken end. I'll use this, Scott thought, as he released the binding. I'll dig myself up into the warm sun.

He stopped in mid thought. Up into the sun? Or down? WHICH WAY IS OUT? He had assumed that up was the way he would dig; but what if that was the wrong way? Wasn't it possible that digging toward his feet was the real way out? Or even sideways?

With new panic, Scott realized it all depended on which way he had landed. He tried to think. Were his eyes facing the center of the earth or the sky? He

35

couldn't tell. Or could he? His mind raced, searching his memory for something he was supposed to know about up and down. There was a word, and he knew that he knew it. It came. *Gravity.* If you dropped something, it would fall toward the center of the earth. And that was down. Simple.

The problem was that Scott had nothing to drop and nowhere to drop it. And no way to see where it landed. The disappointment brought more panic, making him dizzy, sick. He swallowed to get rid of the bitter taste in his mouth. And he had the answer. Spit. SPIT! He laughed out loud, and the sound was eaten by the snow.

He scooped snow into his mouth. The snow melted, but before he could open his mouth to let it out, it began sliding down his throat. Toward his stomach. Toward the center of the earth!

Scott knew which way he had landed. He opened his mouth to make sure. The water did not fall out. It slid down, making Scott cough it up. If his stomach was down, then his head was up. He was buried standing up!

He began to dig, very slowly, with the broken ski. Immediately snow fell around his face. This time he didn't panic. He patted the snow away from his head, blowing to make it stick together. He raised the ski and dug again, pushing downward with his feet.

Minutes passed like hours. He talked to himself, kept himself from hearing the voice that was whispering at the back of his mind: It's no good, Scott. . . . This is the wrong direction; you're digging in the wrong direction! Stop, dig over there . . . over there, not this way!

He did stop, only to calm himself, reassure himself. He dug, moved snow away from his face, used hands and elbows to inch himself up, dug more. Ten minutes passed, twenty. . . . It seemed useless; he was getting nowhere. Maybe it was the wrong direction. It would be so easy to dig sideways for a while. His arms ached from the effort of reaching up. And then he saw light. It was very dim, but he saw it!

The ski broke through the surface of the snow. He dropped it and dug with his hands. Sunlight pierced his eyes. A rush of air filled his lungs. He was out!

# 7

## Where Is Tony?

Scott lay on the surface, gulping in the cool air between sobs of relief. He had made it. He wasn't going to die. He was safe.

He swept his eyes across the snow, searching for some sign of Tony. A ski tip, a glove, anything. The sun's brilliance was painful, blinding him.

Tree branches, bits of bark, chunks of rock littered the snow. He crawled on hands and knees to grasp a tree limb, thinking it was an arm.

Then he pulled himself to his feet. Standing, he had a better perspective. The smooth ice cream he and Tony had skied across was gone. He had awakened on a different planet. Now he stood in a field of snow boulders: shoulder-high deposits of ice and dirt-encrusted snow. Tony was under this mass of mountain vomit.

The thought of his brother suffocating under his feet somewhere released strength Scott thought he'd spent.

He yelled. "TONY! TONY!!" He heard his voice bounce off the cliff sides. Somewhere, something crumbled. He whirled toward the sound. He saw only more of the same: piles of jagged, dirty snow.

He snatched up the broken ski and began stabbing at the snow near his escape hole. It was possible, just possible, that he and Tony had landed together. Even as he flung chunks of ice out of his way, he knew it was useless; Tony could be anywhere.

Tears streamed down his face. He dropped the ski and let himself bawl. "Don't let him die, God, please. . . . Don't let my brother die."

He wiped his eyes with bloody fingers. His nails were broken down to the flesh. He looked at his watch. Almost twelve thirty. He remembered checking the time as he and Tony had started to leave the meadow. Then it had been a little after eleven thirty. Fifty-seven minutes. That's how long he'd been buried. And Tony was still under there.

Scott knew he had no choice. He had to go for help, but how could he leave Tony buried here? Tears of frustration stung his eyes. He fought down the panic, the temptation to lie down and bawl again.

He knew it was stupid to stand there. The big hand on his watch had moved to the seven. Tony might be alive and digging himself out at that very second. Or dying under tons of snow.

Scott shielded his eyes and searched for the trail their skis had left in the meadow. Turning his back on the mountain, and on Tony, he started running. A mistake.

Instantly he was knee-deep in snow. He pulled himself out and started again.

It was agonizingly slow without skis. Scott was careful to put his feet on the ski marks. Several times he sank crotch-deep. Sweat dripped from his nose and soaked him under his down jacket. He wanted to throw it away, but stopping was out of the question.

He stopped anyway. A sudden thought shook him. He would have to drive the truck down the mountain. The idea terrified him. What if the truck went out of control? He remembered the S-turns . . . the drops that went down forever. Another stab of fear. What if the truck had been swept away or buried in the snow?

He turned back toward the meadow and screamed, "TONY! PLEASE ANSWER, TONY!"

Only his echo responded.

Out of breath, sobbing, he forced himself to continue. He'd find the truck. He would drive the truck. Go slowly, take your time. Panic kills. Tony was waiting. Maybe he was dead. Maybe not.

The truck was there, pointing downhill as Tony had left it. Had he done that on purpose, aware that something might happen? Scott was glad he didn't have to make a U-turn.

He climbed in, grabbed the keys, found the one that fit the ignition. He turned it, applying his right foot to the gas. The truck coughed, lurched and stalled. Scott stared at the floorboard, dismayed. Inside the cab it was twenty degrees hotter than outside. Sweat ran into his eyes.

He tried again. The same thing happened. He shut his

eyes, tried to remember Tony's feet, what they had done. He turned the key again, this time depressing the clutch instead of the gas. The engine caught and the truck lurched backwards, stalling. It was in reverse. He found neutral, started the engine again and gently slipped into first. The pickup moved forward. He was driving down the mountain.

Scott's mouth was as dry as ashes. Swallowing was out of the question. Bone showed white through skin as he gripped the scorching steering wheel. He didn't feel the hot plastic.

One foot stayed close to the clutch; the other rested on the brake. First gear was all he would dare.

Inches to his left, a chasm dropped out of sight. Scott couldn't look. If he did, he knew he would drive over the edge.

At the first bend, he depressed the clutch and pressed down on the brake. He felt the rear end move slowly toward the edge of the cliff. In desperation he slammed his foot down on the gas pedal as hard as he could, letting up on the clutch with his other foot. The truck roared forward. Scott laughed out loud, giddy with the knowledge that he had saved his own life for the second time. He knew he was going to be all right.

At one thirty, Scott stumbled into the Village Pantry. He was soaking wet and shaking; his hair hung in a matted tangle over his eyes. His voice came in hoarse gasps. "It's my brother. . . . He's buried . . . an avalanche. . . . TONY'S BURIED!"

He remembered little after that. Hands helped him to a seat, covered him with jackets, spooned hot tea into his mouth. Dave Higgins was moving, talking, giving orders. "Billy, call for the dogs. Sue, get the ski patrol. Tell them to get to the meadow on the front of Smuggler. . . . We'll need probes and a litter, blankets, the works. And fast!"

Then he was standing over Scott, talking. "Scott, can you make it? We need you. Can you take us back up the mountain? Show us where Tony . . . where it happened?"

Scott nodded. Of course he could. Smuggler Mountain was stamped into his brain forever. He wanted to talk to Dave, tell him how it was. The horror of knowing you were going to be crushed . . . of knowing your brother was buried . . . of the blackness.

Then he was in the truck, squeezed between Dave and Billy. Dave knew how to stand in a crouch as he forced the pickup over the bumps. Scott felt nothing. He checked his watch. Two o'clock. Tony had been buried for over two hours.

Dave parked and told Billy to wait for the others to arrive. Everything was happening so fast now. Was it possible that Tony had parked here only a few hours ago?

Squeezing past the steering wheel, Scott felt a movement under his shirt. He had forgotten the animal he found in the avalanche. He zipped his jacket higher and climbed out of the pickup.

Dave was waiting. "Lead the way, Scott." For the third time that day, Scott crossed the white meadow. The snow sucked at his feet, making him flounder. It was white quicksand. It wanted both brothers.

# 8

## *The Search*

Another truck lurched into the spot behind Tony's pickup. It carried the dogs. Tugging at their leads, held by their trainers, barking wildly, they scrambled into the meadow.

Scott wondered how this confusion of straining, twisting racket was going to find his brother. Dave told him they were trained to sniff out a human under five feet of snow.

The dogs overtook Scott and Dave, and reached the site first. All six dogs began pawing the snow near Scott's escape hole. At a command, they abandoned that and began to search more systematically.

Dave and the dogs' trainers stood absolutely still. The dogs were to have a few minutes to search without being misled by other human smells. By that time the ski patrol should have arrived with the probes, Dave explained. They were long, thin bamboo rods; a trained hand holding one could detect the difference between a rock and a body under five feet of snow.

Scott felt useless. Where had the time gone? AND WHY WASN'T ANYBODY DOING ANYTHING? Didn't they understand that Tony was buried? Scott bit his lip to keep from crying.

Dave had been watching Scott. He came and pressed an arm across his shoulders, but didn't say anything. There was nothing to say.

Suddenly Scott jumped.

"What's the matter?" Dave asked.

Scott opened his shirt wide enough for Dave to see the little animal. "I found him while I was buried. He was knocked out, so I stuck him in here to keep him warm."

"It's a pika. In the summer they're up here by the millions. What are you going to do with him?"

Scott stroked the small, trembling head with his thumb. "Would he die if I let him loose now?"

"No way. These things burrow like any other rodent, and multiply like them, too. Chances are his family is waiting for him somewhere."

Scott pulled the animal out of the warmth of his shirt. He waited till the closest dog was headed in the other direction and set the pika on the ground. "Go find your family," he murmured. The pika froze for a second, then vanished under the snow.

One of the dogs was staring into the distance. Scott saw six people hurrying toward the avalanche site. It was the ski patrol.

"How can they move so fast?" Scott asked Dave. "I kept sinking."

"Snowshoes. They'd have skied in, but they need their hands free to carry the equipment."

The patrol went into action immediately. One of the women asked Scott where Tony had been when the avalanche hit.

"I don't remember where we were, exactly," Scott answered. "But he was skiing next to me, and I landed there." Scott pointed at the hole, where several of the others were already busy with the probes.

"Did you have the impression that you were being carried by the snow, or did it just land on top of you?" the woman asked.

Scott remembered the feeling that he was being swept along by a powerful wave, out of control. "I think it carried me, but I don't know where I was when it first got to me."

The woman smiled. "We'll figure that out. Thanks."

She and two of the men walked toward the base of the avalanche path. The rest of the patrol were probing the snow around the hole where Scott had crawled out. They were following the path of the dogs.

First the probe would be pushed gently into the snow. If it struck something, the prober would wiggle the probe around, making a larger hole. Then a dog would be called to sniff into the hole. This happened two or three times before the others returned. They'd made their plan.

Everyone was given a probe, even Scott. They stretched themselves in a line from the hole to the edge

of the avalanche deposit. Each person was responsible for probing a ten-foot circle. If the operation were done properly, a path ten feet wide and a hundred and fifty feet long would be searched.

"What if I hit something?" Scott asked. His mouth was dry. This was a nightmare; it had to be. He couldn't be searching for Tony's body with a stick.

"If you feel resistance, push gently. If the probe stops, chances are it's a rock or tree. If it gives, call one of us fast." Dave showed Scott how to insert the probe, then took his own position in the line.

From above, it would have looked like some weird dance ritual. Fifteen men and women, each holding a long staff, turning in slow circles, poking at the ground. The dogs had given up their own circling and were now mingling with the dancers.

No one spoke. The only sounds were the squeak of leather on snow and the occasional whine of a dog.

Scott was tired. His legs tingled from weakness. They would have buckled if he had been able to relax.

Something broke the rhythm. The dance ended. Everyone stared at the woman who had questioned Scott earlier. She stood still, both hands on the probe, moving it gently back and forth. Quietly, almost in a whisper, she called the nearest dog. The dog sniffed; then, looking up at the woman, began a soft whine.

As if this were a signal, all the dogs gathered around the woman. They too whined, staring at her, waiting. Then the wait was over. She gave the command. "DIG!"

What happened next was a blur to Scott, who had stood frozen since the first dog's whine. Folded shovels came out of packs; the litter was assembled and covered with blankets; snow flew through the air as dogs and humans dug as fast as the tight circle allowed.

Even when Tony's body was carefully lifted out of the hole, there was no talking. In an instant he was on the litter. Scott watched a ski patroller lower his face, glowing with health, over the deathly blue of Tony's. He heard him blow a breath between Tony's purple lips, saw him force air out of Tony's motionless chest.

Scott retched. Turning away, he vomited into the debris around him.

# 9

## *Alive!*

Tony was alive.

Scott watched as the color of his face went from blue to white to almost tan. The mouth-to-mouth resuscitation took only minutes, but to Scott it seemed forever.

His left leg was broken. The jagged end of a broken bone stuck through a bloody gash in his jeans. Someone tied a rubber strap around his thigh to stop the bleeding. A snapped probe became a splint. Tony screamed as the litter strap was tightened over his legs. It was the first sound he had made.

The procession moved across the meadow one more time: six dogs, fifteen people, and their motionless cargo under a mound of blankets. They traveled slowly, knowing that the smallest jolt would be excruciating to Tony.

A white van served as the ski patrol ambulance. Inside there were seats enough for six people and room for a narrow bed. Tony was transferred and strapped down. One of the ski patrollers rode back with Dave and Billy to make room for Scott in the van. The caravan began its descent.

Scott sat near Tony. He had been given a hypodermic for pain. His eyes fluttered each time the van went over a bump. A foolish grin came and went, like the sun on a cloudy day.

"Hey, little brother," Tony whispered. "How're you doing?"

Scott immediately choked up. Damn, why was he always blubbering? "Fine," he managed to say. "How do you feel?"

"How do I look?"

Scott grinned. "Terrible."

"That's how I feel," Tony said. "Where are we?"

"On our way back to town. They've got a helicopter to take you to the hospital."

Tony's grin softened, his eyes closed, and he slept.

A half hour later the van pulled up to the helicopter on the town ball field. About a hundred people crowded around as Tony's sleeping form was carried from the van and tucked into the chopper.

Scott saw Dave talking to the pilot. They were looking at him. Dave ran over and pulled out his wallet. "Here's thirty bucks. It's for tonight and the bus trip back. Good luck."

"What do you mean? Where am I going?"

"To Denver, where do you think?" Dave said. "You don't suppose we're going to send T off to the big city

alone, do you? There's a bus back here tomorrow morning at nine. Be on it."

"Where will I sleep?" Scott asked.

"I'm sure you can stay at the hospital. Ask the nurse to put an extra cot in Tony's room."

Scott took the money, smiled like a fool, and ran toward the helicopter. The copilot yanked him up, and the door slid shut. Snow flew into the crowd as the blades sliced through the air.

Seconds later they were over Smuggler Mountain. Scott pressed his face against the window, trying to see where the avalanche had come down. He saw the peak, but everything else was a blur.

The helicopter arched and thudded into the late afternoon sunlight.

# 10
## Home

Scott was packed. The apartment was straightened up. He looked around. Something wasn't right. A nagging little thought kept inserting itself into his plans for the morning: pack for home, clean the apartment, have breakfast with Dave at the Pantry, drive to the hospital to say good-bye to Tony on the way to the airport.

Of course Scott knew what was wrong. He wasn't going home, because he *was* home. This little apartment already was more of a home to him than the five-bedroom place he'd left in Connecticut. It had taken only a few days for Scott to figure it out. Home was where you were wanted. Period.

He knew he was wanted in Aspen. He didn't know what to expect at his parents' house in Connecticut. He'd find out in about twelve hours.

The lock clicked behind Scott, and he hurried down the steps. Dave had told him to leave his gear on Tony's balcony until after breakfast. They'd swing by and pick it up on the way out of town. Right now Scott wanted fried eggs and homemade toast.

The ride to Denver was long, and Scott talked almost all the way. Dave had a way of guiding a conversation so he became the listener. Scott thanked Dave for spending his free time with him after Tony went to the hospital. He told Dave how he'd felt when Tony left home, about how he hated boarding school, about the divorce. When he finished talking, he felt better.

Dave said nothing for a while; then, in a soft voice, he began to talk. "Seems like a lot of bad things have happened to you, Scott. Big brother runs away, parents stick you in school away from home, parents decide to split up. All bad things, Scott, but none of them really have anything to do with you."

Scott looked over at Dave to see if he was kidding. Nothing to do with him? Who the hell did they have to do with, then?

"Without Tony, without a home, without two parents, you still have the most important thing left," Dave continued. "You have Scott Turner, and he's one hell of a guy. Try not to think about how the world is messing around with your life; think about what you can do to the world." Dave smiled at Scott. "You're going to do just fine," he said. "Now, how about a hamburger before we get to the hospital?"

Tony was dozing when they entered his room. The broken leg was outside the sheet, resting on two pillows. "Looks like the nurses have been writing love poems to T," Dave whispered, pointing to the flowery-looking scrawls on the cast.

Scott giggled. "More likely he's been writing to the nurses."

"How can I get any sleep with you two having a giggling fit?" Tony was glowering at his two guests. "Did you bring me any decent food? They're starving me in here."

Scott handed over the milk shake he'd brought. "Chocolate okay?"

"At least someone is thinking about me. Thanks, Scottie." Then Tony stared at his brother for a long time. "Skater told me you drove the truck down the mountain to get help."

Scott blushed. "Yeah, nothing to it when you know how." Their laughter brought a nurse on the run.

"You boys will have to be quieter. There are sick people in this hospital, too, you know."

Tony winked at Scott. "When do you go back home?" he asked.

Scott smiled to himself. Home. He would be back in Connecticut tonight, but he was home already. "In about an hour. My gear's in Skater's car."

"You mean you're leaving? Now? We haven't done half the things I planned!" Tony looked genuinely disappointed.

"We can do them next time. I mean, well, I want to come back, Tony."

Tony grinned like he'd won the lottery. "When?"

"I was thinking, if it's okay with you, I could come this summer for a week or two," Scott said.

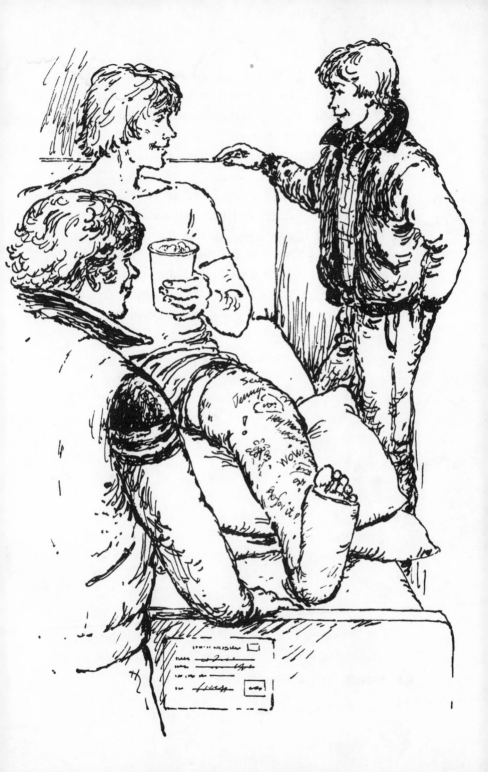

Tony's grin vanished. "It's not okay with me. Either you come for the whole summer or don't bother."

"You got yourself a deal!" Scott let out a howl that got him and Dave evicted from Tony's room. Scott shook his brother's hand, embarrassed. "See you, Tony."

"See you, Scottie." Tony faked an enormous yawn. "Now get out of here so I can get some sleep. There are sick people in this hospital, too, you know."

Dave hurried Scott out the door. "We've got thirty-seven minutes to make your flight," he said.

"No problem," Scott said. "The way I feel right now, I can fly to Connecticut without the plane."